Charles *of the* Wild

John and Ann Hassett

HOUGHTON MIFFLIN COMPANY BOSTON

1 9 9 7

for Nana Martin

Walter Lorraine *wl* Books

Library of Congress Cataloging-in-Publication Data

Hassett, John.
    Charles of the wild / by John and Ann Hassett.
      p. cm.
    Summary: A pampered city dog longs for the freedom of the wild.
    ISBN 0-395-78575-8
    [1. Dogs — Fiction.]   I. Hassett, Ann (Ann M.).   II. Title.
    PZ7.H2785Ch   1997
    [E] — dc20   96-9646
                                                          CIP
                                                           AC

For information about this and other Houghton Mifflin trade
and reference books and multimedia products, visit The Bookstore
at Houghton Mifflin on the World Wide Web at
http://www.hmco.com/trade/.

Printed in the United States of America
HOR   10 9 8 7 6 5 4 3 2 1

Charles
of the
Wild

At number 9 Belknap Street lived a small white dog.
His name was Charles. Charles was not allowed outdoors.
The lady who owned him was forever worried that
he might catch cold.

For those occasions when Charles required a
new suit or needed his fur bathed and powdered,
he was carried to his appointments so he
would not soil his paws. This made Charles
a moody dog.

At breakfast, luncheon, and dinner, Charles
only nibbled. Bitter medicines were spooned
to him three times a day.

Charles had a collection of the choicest dog toys,
but he never played with them. He chewed
the lady's shoes instead—sometimes six or
seven pairs a week.

Only in his dreams was Charles a happy dog.
He hunted rabbits with sharp-nosed foxes.
He howled with coyotes at a pale moon.
He ran swiftly through forests with wolves.

One night Charles could not sleep.

He came upon an open window.

He sniffed for smells of the wild.

Did he hear the far-off calling of wolves?

Charles scurried down the narrow street.

He hoped to find a pack of foxes.

Charles roamed the night. He lost his handsome
lamb's wool sweater. He searched dark
alleys for rabbits and found a snarling flash of
fur instead. He hid at the bottom of a
rubbish bin. Charles howled up at a streetlight
he mistook for the moon.

The next morning, a man dressed in two raggedy old coats appeared. He shared part of a jelly doughnut with Charles. Charles thought it was delicious.

Charles followed the man across a busy street.
They walked four blocks north and three blocks

east and two blocks south and one block west
till they came to the gates of a great city park.

Charles rushed in looking for wolves.

He found only squirrels.

Charles drank from puddles. On the ground
were all sorts of tasty things to eat.

Charles fetched sticks that the man tossed for him.
He rolled in the dust. He dug in the dirt.
He raced the wind and chased a paper bag
all around the park.

It was growing dark when the man and the dog crossed a busy street. They walked one block east and two blocks north and three blocks west and four blocks south until they came to number 9 Belknap Street.